KU-499-713

James Mayhew
presents

Ella Bella
BALLERINA
~ and ~
# The Sleeping Beauty

For Eloise
— Ella Bella —

Thanks to Liz Johnson and Tim Rose for their vision and inspiration,
and to Kate Burns for giving me the idea.
And thanks to Anglia Ruskin University in Cambridge
for offering a research grant.
J.M.

ORCHARD BOOKS
338 Euston Road, London NW1 3BH
Orchard Books Australia
Level 17/207 Kent Street, Sydney, NSW 2000

First published in 2007 by Orchard Books
First paperback publication in 2008

ISBN 978 1 84616 299 2

Text and illustrations © James Mayhew 2007

The right of James Mayhew to be identified as the author and
illustrator of this book has been asserted by him in accordance
with the Copyright, Designs and Patents Act, 1988.

A CIP catalogue record for this book
is available from the British Library.

5 7 9 10 8 6 4

Printed in China

Orchard Books is a division of Hachette Children's Books, an Hachette UK company.
www.hachette.co.uk

James Mayhew
presents

Ella Bella
· BALLERINA *·*
~ and ~
The Sleeping Beauty

ORCHARD BOOKS

Ella Bella loved Madame Rosa's ballet class
at the old theatre.

The lessons were always fun. Ella Bella's
favourite part was when they danced to the music
from Madame Rosa's marvellous musical box.

One day, Madame Rosa said,
"My darlings, let us listen to the music
from *The Sleeping Beauty* ballet.
I want you all to imagine
you are fairies!"

Madame Rosa opened the box and sparkly music filled the air. The little ballerina inside the box began to twirl, and Ella Bella and her friends danced like pretty fairies.

"Please tell us the story of Sleeping Beauty," said Ella Bella.

"Well," said Madame Rosa, "her name
was Princess Aurora and she was born
in a fairytale palace . . ."

"Princess Aurora's christening was a joyous event. Good fairies gathered and bestowed gifts of beauty and grace. But then, disaster! The bad fairy arrived. Furious not to be invited to the palace, she cast an evil spell – on her sixteenth birthday, Aurora would prick her finger on a spindle and die!"

"How terrible!" gasped the children.

"Ah, but the kind Lilac Fairy still had a gift to give," smiled Madame Rosa. "She changed the spell so that Aurora wouldn't die, but would sleep for a hundred years, only to be woken by a prince's kiss!"

"And did the prince come?" asked Ella Bella.

"My dear, there isn't time for the whole story today," smiled Madame Rosa, closing the musical box. "It's nearly home time."

The other children went to get their coats, but Ella Bella stayed behind on the stage . . .

When she was quite
alone, Ella Bella
opened the musical box.
Just like magic, the
music started and
Ella Bella found she
was dancing . . .

The music seemed to surround Ella Bella,
then a tiny lilac light lit the musical box.
It grew brighter and brighter until
Ella Bella saw a fairy floating towards her!

"I'm the Lilac Fairy," she smiled. "Shall we go?"
"Go where?" gasped Ella Bella.
"To Princess Aurora's sixteenth birthday party,
of course," said the Lilac Fairy.

The Lilac Fairy led Ella Bella
into a palace garden, and there
was Princess Aurora!

As she danced, everyone agreed that she had grown to be the most beautiful princess they'd ever seen. But then an old woman shuffled out of the shadows with a gift for Aurora – a spindle!

Ella Bella remembered the bad fairy's spell. "Don't touch it!" she called.

But Aurora didn't hear. She graciously took the spindle and danced.

Suddenly, she pricked her finger!

Aurora's dance became faster and faster,

until she fell to the floor!

The old woman threw off her cloak. It was
the bad fairy! She vanished in a flash before
anyone could catch her.

"Carry Aurora to the tallest tower," said
the Lilac Fairy sadly. "There she will sleep
for one hundred years."

"But what about everyone else?" wondered
Ella Bella.

"We'll put a spell on them too," whispered
the Lilac Fairy.

Ella Bella took the Lilac Fairy's
hand and they began to fly.
It was like dancing in the air!
They sprinkled a spell over
the whole palace, and soon
everyone had fallen fast asleep.

Roses began to grow up the tallest tower, where Aurora slept, and around the palace a magic forest grew.

"When will the prince come?" asked Ella Bella. "Will we have to wait one hundred years too?"
The Lilac Fairy laughed. "Not with a little more magic!" And as she waved her wand, one hundred years raced by . . .

Ella Bella saw they were now
in another kingdom. A dashing
prince was riding towards them.
The Lilac Fairy told him the
sad tale of Princess Aurora,
asleep in the tower.

"Will you help her?" asked Ella Bella.
"Of course," said the prince. "It would
be an honour."
"We'll show you the way!" said Ella Bella.

They led the prince to the magic forest. He
slashed through the rose briars with his gleaming
sword. Even though the thorns tore at him, he
didn't stop until he found Aurora's tower.

Gently, he kissed Aurora, and slowly,
softly she opened her eyes and smiled.
It was love at
first sight.

As soon as Aurora awoke, the magic forest
vanished and the whole palace leapt back into life.
"I love it when my spells work," said the
Lilac Fairy. "Let's take a peep at their wedding!"

What a wedding it was!
There was music and feasting, with guests
from all corners of the fairytale kingdom!
"Thank you for your help," said the Lilac Fairy.
"Now they'll live happily ever after!"

"Thank you for a magical time!"
said Ella Bella.
The Lilac Fairy lifted her
wand once more and
the palace was filled with
lilac light and swirling music . . .

Then suddenly the music stopped, and Ella Bella found herself alone on the dark stage. She gently closed the lid of the musical box.

"There you are!" said Madame Rosa, giving Ella Bella her cape. "Your mamma is waiting."
"Can we listen to your musical box next time?" asked Ella Bella.
"Of course," said Madame Rosa. "We'll play a different tune, shall we?"
"I'd like that!" said Ella Bella.

And, humming as she went, Ella Bella danced
with her mamma all the way home.

The Sleeping Beauty is one of the most popular ballets. It was first performed in 1890 at the magnificent Mariinsky Theatre in St Petersburg, Russia. Many spectacular ballets were created there, and their dazzling Russian dancers became famous all over the world.

The music for *The Sleeping Beauty*, written by Piotr Tchaikovsky, is full of glorious melodies, some of which are very well known.

It is exciting to go to the ballet. The music, played by an orchestra, and the theatre, stage sets and costumes are often very beautiful. But it is the dancers that really bring magic and wonder to the performances. They have to work incredibly hard, dancing each step perfectly to tell the story in exactly the right way. Every step, expression and hand movement has a different meaning and so it is possible to tell a story without any words being spoken. Tchaikovsky's music also helps to tell the tale.

The Sleeping Beauty ballet is based on the story *The Beauty in the Sleeping Forest*, an old French fairy tale by Charles Perrault. Tchaikovsky liked fairy tales so much that he added some other characters to Princess Aurora's wedding, including Cinderella and her prince, Hop-o-My-Thumb, Puss-in-Boots, The Blue Bird, and even Little Red Riding Hood, who dances with a wolf! Did you spot them in the wedding picture earlier in the book?